RAPTOR

THE LIFE OF A YOUNG DEINONYCHUS

by **Michel Henry**

illustrations by **Rich Penney**

ABRAMS BOOKS
FOR YOUNG READERS
NEW YORK

The time is more than 100 million years ago.
There are no humans or other large mammals
yet. The world belongs to the dinosaurs.

In an ancient forest of what will become North America, *Deinonychus* naps in the sun. After the recent rains the warmth feels good on the young raptor's damp feathers.

Deinonychus is not the only one who wants the warm spot in the sun.

"SQUAWK! SQUAWK!"

Deinonychus is awakened by the racket. Another raptor
with a funny stripe down its back paces in front of him,
its arms raised in a fierce display of feathers and claws.

Deinonychus is fierce, too, and will not easily
give up his spot. He leaps to his feet, and the
two circle each other, hissing.

Then, "*GRRRR . . .*"

A familiar deep rumble stops
them both in their tracks.

Top Feather, the leader of their pack, wants the spot, too. And what Top Feather wants, he gets. *Deinonychus* and Stripe retreat. They will both have to find other places to sun themselves.

Days pass. The rains
come less often now.

Deinonychus and the other males
start to have odd feelings inside.
The mating season has begun.

Deinonychus selects a nesting site. Now he must attract a mate. He stretches out his neck and bellows. A female raptor answers him. When she appears, he fluffs out his feathers.

He struts back and forth for hours, trying to show her that he is the best mate for her. By the end of the day, she has moved in. Before long, she will lay her eggs here.

A few weeks later, *Deinonychus*'s mate
sits on a buried clutch of eggs.

One morning, she senses danger. Her
sharp eyes catch a movement in the trees.
A small mammal, a *Gobiconodon*, is
hungry. A raptor's egg would taste good.

But he should know better than to try to steal eggs
when the mother is around.

WHACK! She attacks with such a fury of teeth and
claws, he doesn't know what hit him. She is hungry,
too, and a *Gobiconodon* makes a nice snack.

After two months, the eggs are ready to hatch. *Deinonychus* hears a faint "*squeak–squeak,*" and helps his mate uncover the eggs. Six wet heads appear from the sand, and more are hatching. Ten new raptors enter the world.

The next morning, the hatchlings are hungry.

Born with tiny
teeth and claws,
they are ready
to hunt.

Springing into the air,
they snatch dragonflies.

Pouncing, they catch lizards.

Deinonychus's stomach growls. He can hear *Hypsilophodons* munching ferns in the forest and decides one of them would make a good breakfast.

Hypsilophodons are about the same size as *Deinonychus*, but they are faster.

He sneaks up behind them and picks out a female who is a few yards away from the others.

Lunging at her, he latches on with taloned hands and slashes with the claws on his feet. The desperate *Hypsilophodon* rears up in pain, knocking him to the ground. "*CRACK!*" go his ribs. He is hurt, but she is dying. Before long, *Deinonychus* has his meal.

Two days later, *Deinonychus* is in trouble.
With a cracked rib, it hurts for him to walk or
even breathe. He is hungry, but he cannot hunt.

The other raptors attack and kill a *Tenontosaurus* eight times their size. All he can do is watch.

Deinonychus is lucky this time. The *Tenontosaurus* provides more than enough food, and the hunters have soon eaten their fill.

Careful to stay clear of Top Feather and Stripe, *Deinonychus* limps in to gulp down the scraps. Baby raptors come out of their hiding places and join him.

Three years pass. *Deinonychus* has long since healed, and his babies are now full-grown hunters. One day, at the edge of the forest, *Deinonychus* sees a herd of *Pleurocoelus*. They are enormous and block his view of the sky. Suddenly, a sick one stumbles and falls.

In a flash, *Deinonychus* dives at it through the whirl of dust and giant legs. The other raptors follow close behind, leaping on the downed animal. Though dying, it is still dangerous.

All of them slash with their great claws until the giant plant-eater is finally dead. The raptors prepare to feast.

They tear at the carcass, gobbling down the fresh meat. *Deinonychus* glances nervously over his shoulder as he eats. What was that? He hears a crackling from the forest.

A mighty *Acrocanthosaurus* has been watching them. Roaring, the 6,000-pound monster charges in to claim their meal.

Deinonychus and the others recognize the danger and flee, but an even greater danger lurks in the distance.

The raptors run more than a mile away from the *Acrocanthosaurus*, but *Deinonychus* still hears the crackling in the forest. It is louder, and now he smells smoke. A bolt of lightning from that morning's thunderstorm has caused a forest fire!

Ancient instincts take over as *Deinonychus* and the other raptors scatter in terror. Before he knows it, smoke is everywhere, and he has lost sight of the others.

Flames lick at his feet and singe his feathers as he runs, but luck is with him once again. Suddenly, the wind shifts, and the fire retreats. *Deinonychus* is saved, but in another part of the forest Top Feather and other raptors die in the smoke and fire.

Two days later, *Deinonychus* has located some of the surviving raptors from his pack. They are all hungry and weary from their flight. A light breeze blows, and *Deinonychus* sniffs a welcome scent. He and the others follow it to a decaying *Eolambia* carcass.

When they get there, they find Stripe and others from their group already feeding.

The two groups circle and hiss at each other. Without Top Feather, the raptors are uneasy. They will not survive long without a leader.

Deinonychus approaches Stripe and challenges him. Raising his arms and spreading his feathers, he looks ferocious. Stripe hisses back and they charge at one another. The two battle until both are bloody, and Stripe can fight no more.

As a cooling rain begins to fall, *Deinonychus* turns his attention back to the *Eolambia* carcass. He invites the others to join in the meal. He must take care of the pack now, for *Deinonychus* is their new leader.

Deinonychus has won.

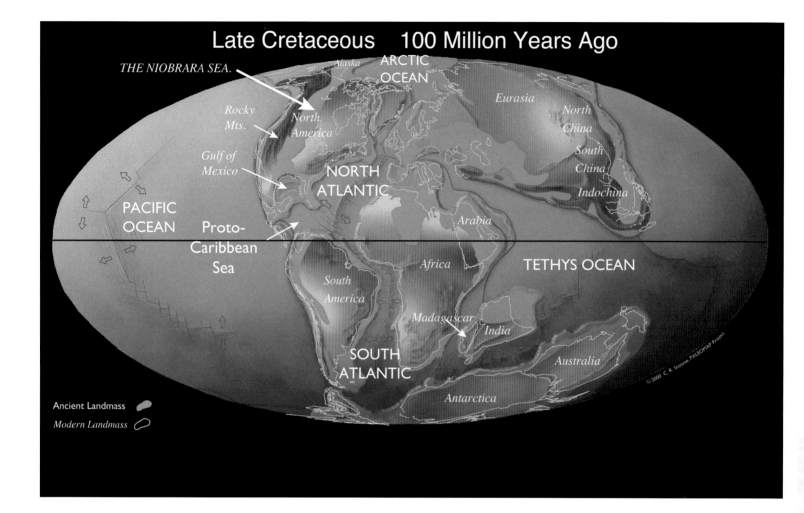

The Cretaceous Period lasted from 146 million years ago until 65 million years ago. This map shows how the landmasses of the planet looked at the time of our story, 100 million years ago. The white outlines denote the modern shapes of the continents as we know them today.

Our story takes place in North America, in the great forest that existed beyond the western shore of the great inland sea called the Niobrara. The fossil remains of several different kinds of dinosaurian raptors—including *Deinonychus*—have been discovered here.

GLOSSARY

Acrocanthosaurus (ack-row-CAN-thuh-SAWR-us): a large meat-eating dinosaur that lived in western North America, *Acrocanthosaurus* grew to a length of 30 to 40 feet. This two-legged hunter had long, strong arms that ended in three-fingered hands with sharp claws.

Carcass: (CAR-kiss): the dead body of an animal.

Clutch (klutch): a nest of eggs.

Decaying: rotting.

Deinonychus (DIE-non-i-kus): a two-legged, meat-eating dinosaur that lived in North America during the Cretaceous Period, about 100 million years ago. It grew to a length of 8 to 10 feet. *Deinonychus* had a curved claw on one toe of each foot that it used as a deadly weapon.

Eolambia (ee-oh-LAM-bee-uh): a four-legged, plant-eating dinosaur. One of the "duck-billed" dinosaurs (which are also called Hadrosaurs). It was discovered in 1997. It, too, lived in western North America about 100 million years ago.

Gobiconodon (go-be-CON-uh-don): one of the earliest meat-eating mammals, it first appeared about 140 million years ago. This predator grew to the size of a large house cat.

Hatchlings: animals newly hatched from eggs.

Hypsilophodon (HIP-so-LOFF-uh-don): *a* swift-moving, two-legged, plant-eating dinosaur. It grew to a length of 6 to 7 feet and lived in western North America in the early Cretaceous Period. It had a horny beak, strong jaws, and teeth made for grinding plants.

Mating season: that time of year when male and female members of the same species are instinctively drawn together to choose mates and have babies.

Pleurocoelus (ploor-uh-SEE-lus): a Sauropod, or giant, plant-eating dinosaur, which grew to a length of at least 60 feet. It lived in western North America about 100 million years ago.

Raptor (RAP-tor): small to midsize two-legged, meat-eating dinosaurs. Most raptors had a sickle-shaped, retractable claw on each foot, used for slashing their prey.

Taloned (TAL-und): having talons, or claws; usually found on meat-eating animals and used for wounding or capturing prey.

Tenontosaurus (ten-ON-tuh-SAWR-us): a plant-eating dinosaur with a long tail, sturdy back legs and long, thinner front legs. It may have been able to walk on its hind legs, but probably ran on all four. It lived in western North America about 100 million years ago.

SELECTED BIBLIOGRAPHY

Bakker, Robert T. *Raptor Pack*. New York, NY: Random House Books for Young Readers, 2003.

Currie, Philip J., and Kevin Padian. *Encyclopedia of Dinosaurs*. San Diego, CA: Academic Press, 1997.

Due, Andrea. *Dinosaur Profiles: Deinonychus*. Farmington Hills, MI: Thomson Gale, 2004.

Farlow, James O., and M.K. Brett-Surman (editors). *The Complete Dinosaur*. Bloomington, IN: Indiana University Press, 1999.

Fritz, Sandy, and George Olshevsky. *Velociraptor*. Mankato, MN: Smart Apple Media, 2003.

Lessem, Don. *Raptors! The Nastiest Dinosaurs*. New York, NY: Little Brown & Co., 1996.

Martin, Anthony J. *Introduction to the Study of Dinosaurs*. Oxford, UK: Blackwell Science, 2001.

Norman, David. *Dinosaurs*. New York, NY: Prentice Hall, 1991.

Parker, Steve. *Dinosaurus: The Complete Guide to Dinosaurs*. Ontario, Canada: Firefly Books, Ltd., 2003.

Paul, Gregory (editor). *The Scientific American Book of Dinosaurs*. New York, NY: St. Martin's Griffin, 2003.

Prum, Richard, and Alan Brush. "Dinosaur Feathers." *Scientific American*, March 2003.

Sloan, Christopher. *Feathered Dinosaurs*. Washington, DC: National Geographic Society, 2000.

Troll, Ray, and Bradford Matsen. *Raptors, Fossils, Fins and Fangs*, Berkeley, CA: Ten Speed Press, 1998.

Weishampel, D.B., P. Dodson, and H. Osmólska (editors). *The Dinosauria*. Second edition. Berkeley, CA: University of California Press, 2004.

Zimmerman, Howard. *Dinosaurs! The Biggest, Baddest, Strangest, Fastest*. New York, NY: Atheneum Books, 2000.

ARTIST'S NOTE

Before I begin to paint a project such as *Raptor*, there are many questions I need to ask. How did a dinosaur like *Deinonychus* look when it was alive? What did it eat? What kind of environment did it live in? What kind of animals lived alongside it in the same place at the same time, and how did *they* look when they were alive?

I begin my research with books (see the Selected Bibliography). Then I meet with my longtime friend and consultant, paleontologist Tom Williamson. I then seek out and study actual fossils of the animals I'm going to illustrate. This may entail online research, or visiting museums, or asking paleontologists for copies of photos of fossils they have worked on.

We know that *Deinonychus* was a swift animal because of the structure of its leg bones. We know that it was a predator based on its sharp, meat-cutting teeth. There is evidence that raptors hunted in packs, including fossil remains of a group of raptors that attacked and killed a *Tenontosaurus*, a fairly large "duck-billed" dinosaur. We don't know for sure that *Deinonychus* had feathers, but there is reason to believe it did. *Deinonychus* is part of a dinosaur family called Dromaeosaurids. All raptors are part of this family, and several other kinds of raptors have been found to have feathers. The most recent discovery in this group is *Microraptor gui*, a small, Chinese dinosaur whose fossils had the impressions of feathers on both its arms *and* its legs.

There is also the question of whether or not raptor parents cared for their young after hatching. While there is no direct evidence for this, more and more paleontologists are accepting the idea. Alligator moms care for their hatchlings. In many bird species both mother and father care for the hatchlings until they can fly and are ready to leave the nest. Since birds and reptiles are the dinosaurs' closest living relatives, it is logical to think that at least some predatory dinosaurs, if not all, cared for their young until they were ready to hunt and kill food on their own.

The final consideration for painting is color. We have no idea what colors the dinosaurs were. But, once again, we have living relatives, like reptiles and birds, to use as examples. Looking at them, we can see that many birds and reptiles are brightly colored and many of them are also multicolored. Painting dinosaurs in bright colors makes people stop and think about how they might actually have looked when they were alive. We don't know if it's right or wrong, but it makes more sense than thinking that all dinosaurs were either gray or brown, which is how they were painted during the first half of the twentieth century.

Editor: Howard Zimmerman
Designer: Gilda Hannah
Production Manager: Alexis Mentor

Library of Congress Cataloging-in-Publication Data:
Henry, Michel, 1962–
Raptor : the life of a young deinonychus/ by Michel Henry ; illustrated by Rich Penney.
p. cm.
ISBN-13: 978-0-8109-5775-6
ISBN-10: 0-8109-5775-2
1. Deinonychus—Juvenile literature. I. Penney, Rich, ill. II. Title.

QE862.S3H46 2006
567.912—dc22
2004012588

Printed and bound in Singapore
10 9 8 7 6 5 4 3 2 1

A Byron Preiss Book

HNA
harry n. abrams, inc.
a subsidiary of La Martinière Groupe
115 West 18th Street
New York, NY 10011
www.hnabooks.com